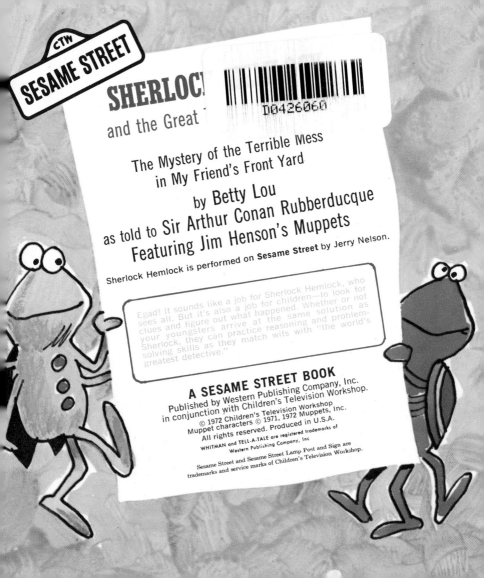

SESAME STREET CTW

SHERLOC[K]

and the Great T[...]

The Mystery of the Terrible Mess
in My Friend's Front Yard

by Betty Lou
as told to Sir Arthur Conan Rubberducque
Featuring Jim Henson's Muppets

Sherlock Hemlock is performed on **Sesame Street** by Jerry Nelson.

Egad! It sounds like a job for Sherlock Hemlock, who sees all. But it's also a job for children—to look for clues and figure out what happened. Whether or not Sherlock, they can practice reasoning and problem-solving skills as they match wits with "the world's greatest detective."

A SESAME STREET BOOK

Published by Western Publishing Company, Inc.
in conjunction with Children's Television Workshop.

One day, as I walked past my friend's house, I spied a terrible mess in his front yard.

"What a terrible mess!" I cried. "What on earth has happened here?"

Just then a man in a checked hat and coat appeared carrying a magnifying glass.

"Sherlock Hemlock here, the world's greatest detective," the man announced. "Sherlock Hemlock sees all!"

"Hello!" I said.

The man leaped three feet into the air. "Zounds!" he cried. "I didn't see you!"

"I'm glad you're here, Mr. Hemlock," I said. "Maybe you can tell me what on earth has been happening here."

"Aha!" said the man. "Has something been happening here?"

"Indeed it has," I answered. "There's a terrible mess in my friend's front yard."

"A terrible mess!" said the man. "That
sounds like a job for Sherlock Hemlock."
"Look!" I said, pointing. "There are some
little horns and paper hats. Perhaps they
will help us guess what happened here."

Sherlock Hemlock frowned.

"Now, let me see," he said. "You probably haven't noticed this, but in the front yard there are some horns and paper hats. I've got it! The Twiddlebugs were doing their famous jellybean dance."

"What?" I exclaimed.

"Once every seven years," he said, "the Twiddlebugs appear and play their horns in the hope that it will rain jellybeans. When the jellybeans start raining down, the Twiddlebugs take off their hats and try to catch them."

Now, it seemed to me that there might be a simpler way to explain what those horns and paper hats were doing there. Do *you* think Sherlock Hemlock was right?

"I think there might be a simpler way to explain what those horns and paper hats are doing there," I said. "That piece of cake in the yard tells me something."

"Quiet!" replied the great detective. "Do you see that piece of cake there? When the Twiddlebugs did their jellybean dance, and no jellybeans fell from the sky, the Twiddlebugs got very hungry. They began to eat that piece of cake."

"But how do you explain the candle in the piece of cake?" I asked.

"Egad!" said Sherlock Hemlock. "There is a candle in that piece of cake! That can mean only one thing. While the Twiddle-bugs were doing their dance, along came a big, scary monster who threw candles at them. One of the candles stuck in that piece of cake."

I thought about it. Horns and paper hats, and a piece of cake with a candle in it. Where had I seen those things together before? It certainly wasn't at a Twiddle-bug dance!

I was absolutely sure now that I knew what had happened in my friend's front yard. Can *you* guess what it was?

Then Sherlock Hemlock pointed to some crumpled paper on the grass.

"Aha!" he cried. "When the Twiddlebugs discovered that a big, scary monster was throwing candles at them, one of them wrote a message on that paper. Something like: 'Dear Sherlock Hemlock, please help! A big, scary monster is throwing candles at us!'"

"But, Mr. Hemlock," I said, "that's wrapping paper—the kind you wrap birthday presents in."

"Don't be silly, young lady," said Sherlock Hemlock. "The big, scary monster grabbed that paper and crumpled it up. And he chased all the Twiddlebugs into *that* house. That's it! The remarkable brain of Sherlock Hemlock has solved another mystery!"

"You may be a great detective," I said to Sherlock Hemlock, "but I think you are wrong about why those horns and hats and that piece of cake with a candle in it and the crumpled wrapping paper are in my friend's front yard. I think that what happened here was a birthday party! And I think most people would agree with me!"

"You believe the great Sherlock Hemlock
has made a mistake!" exclaimed Sherlock
Hemlock. "Amazing! But, look, there's your
friend coming out of his house. Why don't
you ask *him* what happened here?"

I waved to my friend.

"Friend," I shouted, "this gentleman and I have been having a little argument. You can settle it if you tell us what has been happening in your front yard."

"Oh," said my friend, "it's very simple. Today's my birthday, and I had a party here."

Sherlock Hemlock shook his head.

"Impossible!" he cried. "No Twiddlebugs doing the jellybean dance? No monster throwing candles? Sherlock Hemlock has never been wrong before! . . . Oh, well, there's always a first time." And, with a sigh, the great detective moved on down the sidewalk.

"Well," I said to my friend, "let's go inside and look at your presents!"

"I'd love to invite you in," said my friend, "but I can't. You see, we were having the party when all of a sudden all these little bugs came and started doing a dance, and then a monster ran up and threw candles at everyone and chased us into the house. You can't possibly go in there now."

"So Sherlock Hemlock was right after all!" I said.

Just then the door to the house flew open and out ran hundreds of screaming Twiddlebugs, followed by a big, scary monster throwing candles at everyone.

"Well, look at that!" I said, thrilled at the fact that I had been there to listen while Sherlock Hemlock, the world's greatest detective, solved perhaps his greatest case—the mystery of the terrible mess in my friend's front yard!